MEERA GODBOLE-KRISHNAMURTHY is the author of *Balancing Act*, a novel that draws unexpected parallels between the practices of architecture and motherhood. She has lived in the Philippines, France, and the United States. She studied art and architecture at Oberlin College and Columbia University, and received a Masters of Architecture from the University of Virginia in 1992. She currently lives in Mumbai and is Editor-in-Chief of *Saffronart*. Her next architecture-based novel is presently under construction.

Gardens of Love

STORIES OF A MARRIAGE

Written and Illustrated by

Meera Godbole-Krishnamurthy

SPEAKING
TIGER

SPEAKING TIGER PUBLISHING PVT. LTD
4381/4, Ansari Road, Daryaganj
New Delhi 110002

Published in India by Speaking Tiger in paperback 2018

ISBN: 978-93-87164-59-8
eISBN: 978-93-87164-61-1

10 9 8 7 6 5 4 3 2 1

Typeset in Bembo Std by SÜRYA, New Delhi
Printed at Sanat Printers, Kundli

For my parents
and to Meow, who once walked among us

Itinerary

Lodhi Garden

*S*pread over ninety acres, Lodhi Garden contains tombs and monuments from the Sayyid (1414-1451) and Lodhi (1451-1526) dynasties who ruled the Delhi sultanate, and a bridge from the early Mughal Empire. The village of Khairpur grew around the structures in subsequent centuries, and the villagers were relocated by the British in order to create the gardens around the tombs. The park was landscaped by Lady Willingdon, wife of the then British Viceroy; hence its original name of Lady Willingdon Park upon its inauguration in 1936. It was renamed Lodhi Garden in 1947 following India's independence from British rule. In 1968, the gardens were relandscaped by architect Joseph Stein. The site is now protected by the Archaeological Survey of India.

The oldest structure in the garden, visible from the street, is the mausoleum of Muhammad Shah Sayyid, the last of the Sayyid dynasty rulers. The octagonal structure was built on a mound in 1444 by Alauddin Alam Shah as a tribute to Mohammed Shah. It is surrounded by royal palms and has a verandah running around it with three arched openings on each of the eight sides.

At the centre of the garden is a set of three buildings built in 1494. The Bara Gumbad, or Big Dome, is shaped like a tomb but has no grave. It is composed of red sandstone ornamentation, arched recess and decorative battlements. It leads to an adjacent richly decorated, three-domed mosque with calligraphy, paintings and decorative plasterwork. The facing pavilion, without a dome and lacking ornamentation, is the Mehman Khana or guest house, probably for pilgrims who visited the mosque.

Directly opposite the Bara Gumbad lies the Sheesh Gumbad, built the same year. Its dome, now mostly bare, was originally embellished with blue enamelled tiles, reflecting Persian architecture.

The youngest tomb in the garden is that of Sikander Lodhi, commissioned by his son Ibrahim Lodhi in 1517. It is also octagonal in shape, like the tomb of Mohammed Shah Sayyid, but is set within a 75-metre square enclosure with fort-like rampart walls. Ibrahim was the last Sultan of Delhi from the Lodhi dynasty—he was defeated by Babur in the first battle of Panipat in 1526, leading to the beginning of the Mughal Empire.

The Athpula Bridge, composed of eight piers originally spanned a tributary of the Yamuna river. Built by Nawab Bahadur, it is one of the few surviving works built in Delhi during the reign of the Mughal emperor Akbar (r. 1556-1605). It was previously called Kairpur ka Pul, after the original village of Khairpur in which it was located.

There is also a six-metre tall, unnamed turret in the Lodhi Garden which was probably one of the corner towers of a large enclosure which no longer exists. It remains undated but is possibly even older than the Tomb of Mohammad Shah Sayyid.

'He Said—She Said'

They had not met in weeks, months, though here, now, it felt like years. It was perhaps a lifetime ago that they had made an appointment to meet at the Lodhi Gardens on this not especially distinct Friday evening. Neither expected the other to show up. He walked into the parking lot at 5:30 pm. He was particular about time—he hated to be late. And he hated to be kept waiting. Out of some old habit, he leaned against the low stone wall beside the Kwality ice cream man, and sort-of-waited. There was no obvious expectation in his distracted gaze as he nibbled at his orange bar. He decided that he would enter the garden in exactly ten minutes. Till then, he watched the daily garden users—so easily identified by their purposeful strides—come and go.

And then he saw her pull up in her white Maruti. She parked it, slightly off the parallel—which also irked him still— and walked towards him. She was particular about time too. She resisted being controlled by it, and never made it to any meeting on time. It upset her psyche.

They said hello as though they had parted only hours ago. It was always this way with them. And then, without much ado, they walked through the dividers and onto the bridge, and into the garden.

Stepping from the tarred parking lot on to the curved surface of the pink sandstone-paved Athpula bridge soothed her, as stone surfaces tended to do. She stopped and took off her shoes while he took photos of the parrots perched on the bridge wall.

'Why do you think this is called the Athpula?' he asked. 'Why count the piers rather than the openings? Why not Satpula, for the seven voids?'

Barefoot, she tried to feel every joint between the randomly cut stone. 'Yes, it would be much more logical. Emptiness holds more possibilities than dense, already formed mass,' she agreed.

They paused to watch the parrots fly away, leaving behind eight empty spaces which would later be filled by the images of their presence in their memories. She walked ahead, eager to feel the next change in texture. He followed, shifting his gaze from parrot green to the varied hues of foliage ahead.

Back on an even surface, she felt the slightly warm tar against her feet as she held her sandals in her left hand. To their right they saw a small domed structure, partly hidden by trees. Any movement they made further obscured it from view. As she stared at the trees which she thought looked threatening, she sensed she was being watched. She turned and found herself gazing into those eyes she knew so well. But that had been a long time ago, and the garden now beckoned. There was still so much more to see, so much more to know. They looked away and walked on.

The gently curving pathway opened up quite suddenly into a circle sixty feet in diameter. Someone they had both once known referred to it as the 'witches circle.' It was a strange space, surrounded by tall bushes, its exit faced only a massive masonry wall. It was quiet within this circle, and they slowed down and stopped. A pause, really, at the very centre of the tarred, seemingly enormous emptiness. Other walkers curved around the two of them, who stood frozen in the centre, and who knows in what moment of their past.

There was no conversation, everyone somehow fell silent in this space. The silence, having once entered their present, would be difficult to shake off. It had had an irrevocable effect on their moods, and it would remain with them through the rest of the evening. As they began walking again, towards what seemed like nothing more than a blank wall, he said, 'Circles never did encourage speech. Not any meaningful speech anyway.'

'Our circles always provoked thought,' she said wistfully. 'Too much thought and not enough speech.'

'Is that why you once said the centre would not hold?' he asked.

But she had already moved on. She did not hear him, though she was just a few steps ahead. And he felt himself much further away from her at that point than the mere ten footsteps which lay between them. He took photos of the spot upon which she had stood only moments before.

Now they arrived at a choice. Left or right. But as always, this decision was about more than direction. Left meant a longer route through the garden, longer walk, more time, more talking, or perhaps longer silences. Going right meant a quicker way to complete the loop and exit, perhaps a brisker pace, shorter conversations, and a quick return to the real world. Both choices also meant entirely different experiences of the garden. Right meant missing out on the grand and largest of the tombs, that of Mohammed Shah Lodhi. So they decided to go left. It was the right thing to do.

But five steps down, they turned around and took a little detour to see the smaller tombs first, with the understanding that they would return to this spot and resume the return to the longer route.

She loved the velvet feel of the lush green grass against her bare feet. He felt rejuvenated by the vast and changing views that greeted him with every slight turn of his head. She led him to the four stone steps leading to the elevated pathway from where she had often stood to look at the Bara Gumbad. How literally it was named, Big Dome. The structure was perfectly set into the wall which held it, ever so gently, it seemed to her, in place. There was a sense of harmony which she found comforting even just to look at. None of this was expressed in words.

He looked to see what she was trying not to say. He saw a well-proportioned stone structure, somewhat eroded by time, which gave it added character. The edges of the building against the still blue sky reminded him of a certain distant evening when their life had been simple and held in place by the mutual joy of being together.

'Not much different than the way the low wall holds this building,' he said out loud.

She was taken aback, but only for a second. Then, ensconced in a known familiarity, they walked over the velvet grass up the steps and into the building.

The darkness provided them shelter from the waning glare of the evening sun. She felt at once calm and comforted by the enclosure of dressed stone—dense and impenetrable. A shuffle in a corner made them realize that someone had already chosen this for his own quiet resting place. They began to feel like intruders. He grew weary, quickly, of the shadowy darkness and turned towards the light. Framed perfectly against the archway was the small, jewel-like Sheesh Gumbad, across the near distance where they had stood moments earlier. The fading sunlight on the dome and the shadows on the west facade made it glow. He was about to ask her to come and stand there dead centre in the opening with him when he felt her take his hand. They stood together, watching in silence as the glow changed shades against the sky which had turned a delicate shade of pink. They imagined the poetry of the blue tiles that had once adorned the now bare Sheesh Gumbad. Words seemed superfluous and the silence was no longer a burden.

She ran down the stone steps, onto the red earth and then into the grass. So many textures and temperatures, all in a rush. He pulled her to stop and look at the facade they were leaving behind. The sculptural quality of the surface with the main arched opening, the relief, the fading and chipped blue tiles, the red and black colours, the steps pulled out of the plane and the play of light and shadow in the evening light. This building was not about death, it was not a tomb.

As they stood appreciating the beauty of the stone form, he once again sneaked a look at her face. She resisted her desire to look at him. She could guess what he was thinking and so instead, she deliberately brushed back her hair with her right hand.

'It hasn't been that long after all,' he said quietly, not knowing or caring whether she heard him.

He pointed, perhaps unnecessarily because she had already focussed on it, to the small niche at the bottom of the steps. It sat there, quietly holding its own in that grand wall face. She touched the single stone which lay at the mouth of the arched niche. 'That cannot have been there since the 1500s,' he said, 'but how eloquently placed it is.'

'It wasn't here the last time I—we—were here. I wonder if someone put it here, and why.'

'Or if it happened to fall, an entirely random happening to which we're now trying to ascribe meaning.'

They looked back at where they had just been. There seemed to be an immensity to the space, but she was thankful for the human scale of the details which were still visible to the eye even from the distance at which they stood. He noticed that the evening was turning softer. A few people sat on the grass now, engaged in conversation. The backdrop of the Bara Gumbad gave the scene a sense of quiet melancholy. Or perhaps he was merely projecting on the visuals again. She was unconcerned by the larger picture right now, too caught up in the details of the moment.

Through the foliage they could see a lonely stone turret—partly hidden from view. He pointed out that it was not partly hidden but rather, partly visible. An important distinction, given their two world views. Getting closer, she looked up at the small, empty balcony.

'Who looked out of there, over what, and for whom...'

'Is it possible that in your melancholic musings you've forgotten to point out the phallic nature of this decrepit form?' he asked.

'That was a long time ago,' she snapped. 'I was young then, too influenced by my overly feminist, liberal education. Now these tiresome, clichéd, associative games bore me.'

'About time,' he said. 'Well, then come look at the eroding stonework... the steps falling apart at the edges... the plants growing in the crevices... entropy...'

'Historians believe this tower predates the oldest tomb in this garden. And yet, here it stands, forlorn and unnamed, the vestige of some past glory. I read that,' she added, pre-empting his question.

Too much looking to the past indicated that it was time to move on, perhaps even move away.

But as they continued their walk, the closeness long forgotten, lost, or perhaps suppressed, began to re-emerge. The brush of a hand, a squeeze on a shoulder, a slight touching of arms, a togetherness of stride. And in this tenuous familiarity they approached another bridge set alongside the cluster of bamboo. It was a narrow bridge, especially with the stream of joggers snaking towards them over it. And so he put his arm protectively around her shoulders as they went over its steep, concrete waffle-tiled surface. They paused briefly against the green tube railing to watch a lone cyclist go past on the bike trail which cut underneath. The bower of trees, the gentle breeze, the lush green garden allowed them, if only for that moment, to exist unencumbered by their own histories, their own and each others' memories and actions.

A linear planting of palm trees directed their vision deeper into the garden and away from the city beyond the wall on their left. The Lodhi Gardens cannot be walked through without pauses unless that is one's predetermined plan. There are too many sights, events, views, details which make one stop—either physically or mentally—to look.

And so their walk continued at an uneven pace because an unplanned walk through the garden had been their only plan. The pauses in their conversation had begun to grow longer again. The quiet had given way to silence. The silence was becoming quietly visible in the periphery, but had not yet intruded on their thoughts.

'Trees which grow up straight and strong out of the earth...' he began to say.

'... but break into pieces against the sky,' she finished for him.

But conversations were inevitable, and soon they were talking about things which circuitously brought back memories perhaps better left undisturbed. Experiences which, though shared, were experienced in separate ways. But then again, they could sense that like this garden, they too did not exist in this present moment alone, but were a collection of their pasts. Times when they had been together yet separate were mixed up with times when they were alone and yet connected to each other. There was much which had been left unexpressed and unresolved, and too much which had been said. This was not the appropriate forum, in the shadow of sixteenth century tombs, nor was it any longer relevant, to clear the past. Yet, the garden in its fullness seemed to draw out of them, certain pain, anger, hurt...

'The palm trees are so perfectly lined. You can almost see the vanishing point,' he exclaimed.

'I see a wall,' she said.

'Look at these grey tree trunks, so tall and proud.'

'I see a road beyond the periphery wall,' she said.

'Listen to the birds,' he cried.

'I hear the sound of traffic,' she said.

'Breathe in the fresh air…' he implored.

'I smell the distant fragrance of pollution,' she said.

'Let's turn around, away from that wall and remain in the garden,' he urged.

The massive tomb of Mohammed Shah Sayyid was right behind them. It was so magnificent that it managed to pull her away from the distant call of the city and back into the garden. They walked around the arcade of the octagonal construction as though circumambulating a religious shrine. They stopped only at an arched opening so she could put her shoes back on. The evening had faded and darkness crept upon them. They walked down the steps around the back and turned to look back. It seemed very large and very old and very alive to her. As though it could see and hear them, as though it wanted to speak of all that it had seen, and withstood and understood over the many centuries gone by.

He drew her attention to the sea of steps they had just descended. Hewn stone, powerful in its fluidity.

'Without stones, there are no steps,' he said, paraphrasing Italo Calvino in *Invisible Cities*.

'I was looking at the cracks in the stones,' she said, not acknowledging the significance of Calvino in their lives at all. 'Cracks large enough to contain an evening.'

'Why do you always look for the emptiness that separates rather than the mass that unites?' he asked almost in exasperation. 'There were hardly any real cracks between us, but you...'

'You're the one who thought the Athpula should have been named for its voids. I only say what I see. And here, now, I see cracks large and strong enough to make me worry about the ability of these steps to hold themselves together. Why do they not fall apart?'

He focussed his camera on one such crack. 'Maybe it's because the stones are leaning on each other to provide just enough support? I wasn't trying to create emptiness, *au contraire*, I was just making sure each of us had enough space to grow...'

He reached for her, but she moved away, off the paved path and onto the grass. But here the grass was brown and their footsteps were loud on the dry leaves that crackled beneath them. They approached a strangely intriguing sight. A small, lonely culvert, just sitting there staring at them while people walked on the paved path that passed over it.

'It's easy to get pulled into that dark, gaping hole. Who knows what lies beyond. Is there light at the end of this small tunnel?' she asked.

'I was looking at the eroding edges around the round blackness. I suppose you'll say that's no different than seeing the cracks in the steps,' he said sadly. 'I'm not sure there is any light there.'

'Stone, concrete, mud, everything does erode and fall apart, I suppose.'

They forced themselves away from the rabbit hole which seemed to be drawing them further into the depths of their despair. And there stood before them a marvellously uninhibited tree, cohabiting with a wild and energetic bougainvillea creeper. It was a sight to behold, they were stunned by the sheer joy of it. And as if to add to perfection, was a bench placed just so, at the base of the tree trunk. There was something extraordinary here. There was a spontaneous harmony about the dishevelled sight and they were, if only for that moment, united in their appreciation for this alternate possibility. Of the reality in which all the pieces were delightfully free and there was joy in the chaos.

The sound of footsteps on dry leaves forced them out of their reverie. A breeze ruffled through the branches of the trees. A few dry twigs fell noisily to the ground. The bench creaked as a tired walker rested on it. They caught snatches of conversations going past in jogging shoes. Then they became aware of each other again, and moved away from that enchanting vision. Even the tomb of Mohammed Shah sighed as they stepped back onto the paved pathway.

They exchanged no words as they followed the path and overtook the occasional walker. They were both wary. In a half-hearted attempt to be frivolous, he stopped at the tree which always made him smile, evoking another memory.

'See the texture of this bark. It's like a woman draped in silken fabric. The creases, the folds, the sensuous fall.'

She could visualize this woman he described and simply nodded.

Further on, they paused at another tree.

'Here's another woman,' she offered. 'This one is dressed in a full skirt. See the folds and gathers? It must be a heavy Rajasthani skirt.'

Somehow, her articulating what he had been thinking didn't seem right. But because he heard the bitterness in her voice, he said, 'She was no more than a friend, I know you know that.'

The *semal* tree was moved by their angst but stood unmoving, rooted to the ground inspite of the fancy skirt, as they walked rather quickly away from it.

Because trees seemed to be a little dangerous for them right now, they decided to stick with the buildings. Up the steps and past the entry court, they found themselves inside a square walled realm. Entering the tomb of Sikander Lodhi was like walking into a self-contained other world. The ordered serenity of the enclosure calmed them. The crenellated stone wall which surrounded them was full of surprises. A corner beckoned and she saw framed views within framed views leading out into an open landscape. Multiple ways of looking at the same thing.

In another corner, he saw a set of steps which lead nowhere. He climbed up and found that he could walk all around the square periphery, contained safely in the thickness of the wall while gazing at spectacular views of the sky above and the garden spread out below.

She leaned against a tree, looking out of the walled enclosure, seeing the same sky and the same garden, but it looked very different from where she stood.

A guard appeared, telling them it was almost closing time. Outside once again, they stayed close to the wall. At each of the four corners of the square was a watchtower. From this perspective outside, it was equally mysterious and forbidding to them both.

The wall had a series of small arched niches at its base and it seemed to go on forever till the next tower made it change direction by a ninety-degree turn. The wall glowed pink and they were once more aware of the other walkers, now mostly headed out of the garden.

As long as they remained beside the wall, square and sure in its geometry, they were safe. Even a mistaken, fleeting glance to the left meant seeing the road, the cars, the security guards, in other words, the city—and reality. That was why they began counting the niches in the wall. They didn't count the individual stones this time.

'Water under the bridge?' he asked.

'You can see that actually there is more water around the bridge than under it,' she said.

'I do see now that the empty spaces are unlikely to be holding up the bridge,' he said. 'It is obviously the piers that bear the load,' he offered.

'I can't see Akbar's Athpula any longer. There seems to be a fog clouding my vision,' she said brusquely.

The fog seemed to have got him too, as his vision blurred as well. The bridge stood there, effortlessly balancing density and emptiness, wisened by the certainty of age.

Parrots squawked, squirrels scampered, a cat sneaked into the brush, and a hundred blackbirds scattered into the darkening sky. Dry leaves cracked underfoot, branches swayed in the wind and a few large, angry raindrops smashed into the pink sandstone walkways, as the garden remained silently watching. They exited into the parking lot, back into the city and the present moment.

But this was not the end of their story. While the physical boundaries of the Lodhi Garden are demarcated by the low wall which surrounds it, there is an experiential, intangible and emotional element to the space which in memory begins only where the actual garden ends.

They would each store and nurture their memories of the garden and their presence in it. Everything now seemed even more unfinished and incomplete than when they had begun their walk and the sky was still blue. They decided to meet again, on another not especially distinct Friday in the future in another place where the physical environment was only a setting for the possibilities which lay hidden in the crevices of time...

Forum Romanum

The Roman Forum is set in the valley between the Palatine and Capitoline Hills of Rome. The site of what are now sprawling ruins, was originally a swampy Etruscan burial ground, and was first developed in the seventh century BC when the land was drained with the building of the Cloaca Maxima, a large covered sewer that flowed into the Tiber river. Over the years, it grew to become the marketplace as well as the centre for the social and political life of the Roman Empire. It is said that it was the place where criminals, sellers of wares, politicians and prostitutes mingled and people from all parts of the world were to be found.

The oldest structure in the forum is the Temple of Saturn (497 BC). Monuments and basilicas were added constantly with emperors trying to outdo their predecessors. The forum developed continuously from the Republican Period through the Imperial Period which began with the principate of Augustus and until the decline of the Roman Empire in the third and early fourth century AD when Constantine I relocated the administrative centre from Rome to Constantinople.

The abandoned forum then fell into decay and was largely buried under debris during the Middle Ages. It eventually became known as the Campo Veccino or cow field. A major earthquake in 847 AD caused considerable damage to several of the remaining Roman monuments in *the forum, which hadn't already been scavenged for building material. During the Renaissance the forum was a stone and marble quarry.*

Archaeological excavation and study of the forum was first conducted by Carlo Fea who concentrated on the area near the Arch of Septimius Severus in 1803. The area was fully excavated only in the early twentieth century and is now the site of massive tourism in addition to the restoration and preservation of monuments that are representative of an enormous span of history.

'He Said—He Said'

*I*t had seemed like a good idea when she suggested it. He knew his father had been hurt by his decision not to remain in the practice. But photography called to him with a seductiveness he could not ignore. He also knew he had disappointed and hurt her by walking out of what was to have been their professional partnership. Along the way, their marriage had taken a hit. It was now his father and his estranged wife who lovingly designed the gardens. He had let them both down. But here, at least, was a chance to make peace with his father. He had been surprised at how quickly he had accepted the offer to spend a week in Rome with him. She had told him his father was lonely, that he was especially lost after the death of his mother last year. She still held it all together for him, he realised with a sudden epiphany. She was his rock. He would languish in solitude without her. He knew where he needed to go after Rome.

But right here, right now, he needed to communicate with his father, and the old patterns began to show up again.

'I can't keep track of this ridiculous listing of names and dates, Dad. Why do you keep up this dull recitation of facts and figures?'

'I'm just trying to teach you a little bit of history. Telling you what I know, and it isn't dull to know facts.'

'Sorry, but I don't care who started which building when and who was succeeded by whom.'

'Ah, it is confusing, isn't it? History always is. And even when we know some things, we never know if what we know is the truth. If what we think happened is really what happened.'

'Then why do you get into it so much?' he asked pointlessly, and then added, 'Oh, never mind. Let's go over there and just appreciate the stones for what they are.'

'Stones? You mean marble.'

'Marble is still stone,' he countered.

'It's metamorphic rock,' his father corrected him. 'Precision, my boy, that's the key.'

'Okay, metaphoric stone it is, then,' he replied, hoping his response had the desired effect on his father. He saw the hint of a smile.

'I remember when we brought you here as a small boy. You were just seven, remember? You loved playing with words then too.'

They were on the Via Sacre, the sacred road that led through the forum.

'Cobbed stones, you would say, no matter how many times I told you it was "cobblestones". It's cobbed, like corn on the cob, you'd explain to us impatiently, with that gap-toothed smile you had.'

He was surprised at his father's precise memory of his tooth-fairy days.

'Well, they do look like giant corn kernels, these cobblestones,' he conceded.

'You still continue to see giants in the most unlikely places? You used to think there was a giant walking past our home when there was thunder.'

'Yeah, I imagine them everywhere and they still terrify me.'

'And you said that shoe house in the Hanging Gardens in Mumbai was just the lost shoe of a giant who roamed the earth trying to find it.'

'Yup, I know. Always waiting for the other shoe to drop. That's me, all right!' He looked at the paved road and ruins surrounding them and saw lots of giants here too—in chariots and togas and sandalled feet. Going to battle and making laws and building temples. 'Giants are seriously bad for self-esteem. It's hard to live up to them. And yet we build our small lives on the shoulders of giants...'

'Precisely! Now you know what I'm talking about. Look at this magnificent road. We walk in the footsteps of giants who came before us and paved the way for us.'

Father and son stood silently as tourists walked by, twisting ankles and straining to push baby strollers. They overheard them cursing the uneven cobblestones and questioning the Roman reputation for road-making.

'All roads lead to Rome, my foot!' someone remarked to responses of, 'Oh god, Dad, that's so lame!' They couldn't help smile at the peals of laughter that followed this exchange.

They arrived at the remains of what had once been the perfectly round Temple of Vesta. The only circle within the straight lines of the forum.

'I like it because it's built in imitation of a primitive hut,' he said, appreciating what was visible of the footprint of the only female sign in this world dominated by the egos of men.

'Where did you get that from? It most certainly isn't. What

primitive hut was a circle? The huts in the Kutch desert of Gujarat, perhaps, but where in the western world? Where do you get your facts.'

'It says so right here, Dad. Just read it,' he snapped, pointing to the guidebook.

'Just because some bozo writes it, doesn't mean it's true,' his father said, impatient with the inaccuracies that threatened to intrude upon his well-constructed world.

'And I don't know, just off the top of my head, yurt, tepee, igloo... But Jesus! Fine, not a primitive hut, you say. Pray, tell us, what is the origin of this round building, then?'

'It was designed as a perfect circle, to represent the sacred, of course. A circle has always been associated with magic and the supernatural. Oddly enough, there was no statue of Vesta, the goddess of home and hearth here, so technically, it wasn't even a temple. It was a sacred building which housed the fire which the six vestal virgins tended to at great risk.'

'A fire which symbolised the perpetuity of the Roman Empire.' He pointed quickly to his guidebook. 'It says so here, it's the bozo again, not me.'

'They lit a new fire on the first day of March every year by rubbing two sticks together. And don't ask me how I know that,' his father said with a smirk, turning up his guidebook-free hands.

'No, they lit it magically by a single, pure ray of sunlight which they could beckon with their chaste beauty.'

'Ah, a bit of the romantic still remains, I see,' his father noted with some satisfaction.

'A building with a vent in the centre of the roof is not conducive to keeping a fire burning eternally. The draft would have put it out too often, wouldn't it?'

'But they needed a perfectly circular building, and without a vent, it wouldn't have been conducive to anyone tending the fire at all, would it, son?'

'The virgins would have suffocated under the pressure of living up to superhuman expectations.'

'No, they would have suffocated because of smoke inhalation,' his dad clarified with precision, looking at his son with a touch of concern.

'Come over here and look at these statues.'

'As long as we don't get into the lives of the virgins and their chastity and the hideous punishments were they to come under suspicion.'

His father said nothing, admiring the classical beauty of the vestals carved in white marble. 'They're all headless, except for the one there. I wonder where the heads are. They must have been stunningly beautiful if that one is any indication of the rest.'

'They were buried alive,' he blurted out, in spite of having just said that they shouldn't discuss the punishments. 'They were buried alive if they slept—or were thought to have slept with anyone.'

'Yeah, let that be,' his father said quickly. 'These statues were dug up in a pile and it's not known how or where they would have been situated originally. This beautiful way they line up and watch us—it's just conjecture that this path would have been so laid out along the courtyard. It's not even clear whether the right statues have been placed upon the correct pedestals.'

'But it's nice that some women were placed on pedestals like men.'

'Yes, but these were not exactly regular women. They were super elite priestesses, their virtues are carved on the pedestals,' he pointed out. 'Almost like female giants, you might say.'

'Those were amazons, dad. That's Greece, not Rome.'

'Yes, of course, another great civilization. But look here. These statues were hewn to fit when they dug them up and decided which one to place on which base. So truly, what we see and think we know now may not even be the true reality.'

'Yes, you're right. They sure look like they're all on the right pedestals though.' He took a few photos, and said, 'Look at the joints. So well fitted. You know what though, dad? The girls who were selected to be priestesses got emancipation from their father's rule. What a relief that must have been.'

His father didn't bat an eyelid. On the contrary he seemed amused. 'Yes, what a relief,' he said. 'They were freed of their fathers and recruited to eternal devotion to Vesta, the goddess of home and hearth. And they had the ability to handle their own property too. So I imagine they must have been quite capable and strong-willed young women to begin with.'

'Here's the Temple of Vespasian and Titus. Father and son. What a pair they must have been. Vespasian died in 79 AD and according to legend his last words were, "Pity, I think I'm turning into a god."'

'What a pretentious twit. They made the laws to deify themselves into gods. It has a name now. It's an illness, dad. They call it delusions of grandeur. What hubris, wasn't that a Roman concept too?'

'Greek,' his father corrected this time. 'His son began construction of the temple to honour his father. And then Titus's brother completed it after Titus died and dedicated it to his father and brother.'

'What was his brother's name?'

'Domitian.'

'Cool name. But I told you I can't be bothered with this listing of father-son, succession mapping.'

'This would be more of a sibling thing.'

But they stood and looked at the temple, or what remained of it, nonetheless—parts of the podium and three forlorn-looking Corinthian columns that hovered together.

Unable to keep it to himself, his father added, after a while, 'Septemis Severus and his son Caracalla made renovations to this temple together, a hundred years later.'

'Caracalla is not a clean-sounding name. No wonder he built the baths.'

'I don't know about that but Caracalla was not very nice. He had his brother killed.'

'No wonder, with that ugly name.'

'Actually, His real name was Marcus Aurelius Antoninus. Caracalla was a nickname based on some kind of Gallic tunic he liked to wear.'

'Sounds like a showy, despotic bad boy.'

'These Thermae Antoninianae must have been spectacular,' his father said, ignoring the pointless comment and looking at the massive ruins with awe writ large upon his weathered face. 'And very popular. The original multi-function social space. Pool, spa, gym, library, gardens, art displays... Domed vaulted ceilings, mosaic walls and floors, and the incredible aqueducts and underground water system. An architectural marvel.'

'So you're admiring what he built and completely disinterested in his despicable politics. It seems he also granted free citizenship to everyone so he could get more taxes.'

'Nothing wrong in that. Citizenship is good for the citizen and the State. Rights and duties—I thought you would appreciate that.'

'I do,' he said, equally impressed by the gigantic arches that lay in ruins around him. 'But what do I know? A nasty guy kills his brother and is remembered only for building something so people could bathe. That's so screwed up.'

His father shook his head and frowned. 'It was considered one of the seven wonders of Ancient Rome. I think you should learn to appreciate the strength of commitment in the world, son.'

'Finally offering me some fatherly advice? It's a bit late for that now,' he said, leading his dad by the arm towards another ruin.

'This, here, is more like it. The Senate. Here, they thought it better not to turn mortals into gods. Got rid of hierarchies.'

'You can't get rid of all hierarchies. You'd have no society then. I'm still your father. I have some advantage on the hierarchy there, no matter the law of every man being equal,' he said.

'It's not about equality.'

'Then what is it about?'

'It's about seeing the other's point of view.'

'And were you pretty good at that with her?'

'All the mistakes weren't mine, you know.'

'They never are, son,' his father said, looking at him with some hope.

'That Caracalla probably walked around this senate in his dumb tunic as well,' was his son's only response.

'Look here, Dad. The Temple of Romulus. His father constructed it to deify his own son. Not the other way around. How's that for hierarchy?'

'This Romulus was not the same as the founder of Rome.'

'So? His father still built him a temple all to himself.'

'That's because he died in battle.'

'So you have to die to have your father cherish you?'

'Everyone fights their battles in life, son.'

'Oh, so you're aware of this. And what do they have to do for some attention from their fathers then? Die?'

'Don't be idiotic,' his father replied, exasperated. 'I've paid attention. I know what's going on.'

'Have you noticed that most, if not all, the structures here were started by one man and completed by his successors? It takes that continuity, it takes more than one man to build something great, to make something meaningful.'

'Yes, yes, I get it. I didn't show any interest in taking over your practice. You seem to be fine building it all alone though.'

'What choice did I have? And anyway, I'm not alone. I have your smart and dedicated wife helping me. She's a great designer, you know. A little too fond of geometry for a landscape architect, though.'

'She likes to be in control.'

'It's a good thing. To want to tame nature, to think ahead, to be thoughtful...'

'You want to talk about this? You want to do this here, now?'

'Son, hush. People are looking.'

'Let them look. I don't know anybody here, I'll never see them again and I don't care what they think. I'm sure they all have their own fathers to deal with.'

'Oh, for crying out loud. You still hold it against me that I wasn't at the dinner table to admire the crayon squiggles you brought home from kindergarten?' his father asked incredulously, eyebrows raised.

'Even my expectations from my own father are cause for disdain to you? You actually don't see the disappointment you caused me and Mom?'

'I thought we agreed before the trip to leave Mom out of this,' his dad said quietly.

'Fine. Leave her to have tended the fire and hearth. You weren't there when I was in kindergarten. You weren't there when I got my report cards in grade school either. Or when I scored a goal in football, or brought home my first girlfriend. Mom taught me to shave, you know. But let's leave her out of it. And you weren't there when my marriage was falling apart either.'

'Oh stop being so dramatic. I worked hard like most professionals, that's all. And all marriages have their ups and downs. You're both fundamentally good people. You'll work it out.'

'Are you being dismissive or supportive, dad? I can't tell.'

'That's always been the problem right there. I've never been dismissive. But you've always been quick to assume the worst about my intentions.'

'Well, I had a childhood full of incidents to lead me to that conclusion,' he said, a little taken aback to realise that he had never given his father the benefit of doubt. 'You never supported me with my photography either. You never even offered to discuss it with me...'

'Stop, stop right there. You never wanted my opinion on anything, ever. Look at this great forum, built by great men. Were they patting their sons on their backs at dinner time? And yet, look at what their sons achieved.'

'But nobody said they were great fathers or husbands... Or great sons,' he added quietly, after a pause.

'What lies before us should teach you something. It is the history of how great civilizations are built.'

'Or, what lies before us in ruins is the anger, resentment and disappointment from centuries of failed father-son relationships, dad.'

'All right, then. If that's what you want, let's discuss this properly. You know what, actually, come on over here to the Rostra.'

'The what?'

'The Rostra. The platform from which the orators gave their speeches. Antony delivered his funeral speech for Caesar here. You like symbolism? You don't care that people are watching? Well, then, don't be shy. Come on, up we go.'

'All right, dad, if that's what you want.'

'No, that's what you want. Drama.'

So they went to the Rostra and had it out. A few people stopped to listen. Not everyone spoke English and not many were interested in watching the family drama they themselves were hoping to avoid at home by making this trip. So father and son continued a dialogue which caused epiphanies, albeit temporary ones, for them both, but generated limited interest among those gathered amidst the ruins to admire a civilization long gone.

'You screwed up your own marriage, son.'

'Well, I didn't exactly have a great role model.'

'When will you take responsibility for your own actions? You can't keep blaming me for the things I didn't do right. Who stopped you from being a good husband to that wonderful wife of yours? Did you stop to think how you were upsetting the life that she had planned for the two of you?'

That stopped him short and so he said nothing. The passage of time had left behind only selective facts that were too difficult to keep track of.

'And before you go judging, let me tell you something else. I knew about every scraped knee and tear and award and love you ever had. Your mom told me everything. I didn't ask you because I asked her. And I cherished every moment of your life in my own quiet way. She understood me, your mom. Selfish as I may have been, she knew I was trying to be the best I could... She did—in that way—tend to the hearth.'

At a loss for words, he sang, 'Lift me like an olive branch, be my homeward dove...'

'We are both of us beneath our love, both of us above,' his father hummed back. Seeing his son's astonishment, he explained, 'Your mother and I had Leonard Cohen long before she shared him with you.'

He settled down on an ancient rock, wondering how many had paused here before him, contemplating the complexities of their lives.

'That's pink granite you're sitting on. It's the decorated base of the column commemorating the father of Constantine. It's the only one that survived.'

'*Possibly*, Dad. It said *possibly*. They don't know for sure who this column commemorated.'

'Well, at least they commemorated somebody, instead of just listing all his faults.'

'Is there anything I've done right? Is there any single thing I've done that lives up to your standards?' he asked at last, unable to contain his exasperation.

'I could ask you the same question, son.'

'Touché.'

'You know, son, at the end of time, this is what remains. Nobody's interested in the small emotions of our miniscule lives.'

'These are not petty matters, dad. They're what life is made of. It's the only thing that really matters at the end of a life. Not these inert stones and broken walls.'

'Nobody can argue about that. But there's more to life than grudges. Especially the ones without a solid foundation.'

'So now my feelings are just unjustified grudges? Because life is so much bigger than my petty emotions?'

'I didn't say petty. Anyhow, history is always complex. We learn what lessons it offers according to our own capacity to understand what transpired.'

'We see what we see, dad,' he said, ending the conversation like so many others that had transpired between them over the years.

'Come sit with me.' His father offered an olive branch once they had walked off some of their gruffness.

'You know she's the one for you, don't you?'

'I don't know.'

'Yes you do, and I do, too. And so does her mom and so did your mom.'

'Didn't know my life was so perfectly clear to all of us.'

'Listen, son. We've all done what we've done. I'm just going to say it now. You forged your own path, that's wonderful. You may not believe me, but I am proud of you. But don't forget to include her in your life. She is smart and wise and loves you in spite of it,' he added with a smile. 'Don't make the mistake I made.'

'You made a mistake choosing mom?'

'No, of course not. But I've made mistakes. Who among us hasn't? Don't repeat them, look before you leap. Don't let her get away.'

'I did let her get away. I already messed it up. The ship has sailed. That story has been written. The road has been traversed. Our paths have diverged. The horse... '

'Stop, I get it. But I told you, we all fight our battles in life. Thankfully, unlike Romulus, you didn't die in your battle. You fight on, you can fix this.'

'What? Like some dumb romantic movie, you want me to go get her back?'

'Yes, that's what I'm saying.' He thought it over for a bit. 'Yes,' he confirmed. 'That's what I'm saying. I haven't let her go far from you, I've held on to her for you, you see. She's there with me in the studio every day, diligently drawing up her gardens of love. Come get her back and fix whatever needs fixing. Fix whatever you think I did wrong too. That's the real father-son bonding we can do here.'

'I should fix your mistakes?' he asked.

His father looked at him and sighed. 'You shouldn't repeat what you think were my mistakes.'

They had wandered back to the massive Baths named after Caracalla—jealous, angry, older brother of the smarter, better-looking, younger Geta—whom he had murdered.

'Legend says Geta bled to death in his mother's arms. Caracalla had tried and failed to kill his own father Severus, too.'

'Rather a bloody history, I agree. Look, son, you may think I did nothing for you, but I do want your happiness. I've held on to her this long for you. She may not want to stay much longer. It's up to you now.'

'Marble may chip and stones may break. People die. But these baths are still here centuries later.' He took the guidebook from his son and read aloud. 'They are a testament to the enduring strength of Roman concrete construction.' At the cost of sounding trite, I would advise you to cement your bonds, like Roman concrete.'

'The Romans sure got that right, didn't they, dad?'

'Yes, son, that they did, indeed.'

Central Park

S et on 843 acres in what is now the heart of New York City, Central Park is America's first major landscaped park. In 1853, the New York State Legislature enacted a law to set aside land on Manhattan Island with the explicit aim of providing a place for peaceful relaxation that would allow city dwellers to enjoy the beauty of 'nature.' Frederick Law Olmsted, already park superintendant, and British-born architect Calvert Vaux, won the 1858 design competition for Central Park, with their Greensward Plan.

Central Park is the result of the collaborative genius of Olmsted's aesthetic vision and Vaux's practical mind. It is generally accepted that Vaux was responsible for all the design work in the park, which includes built structures such as the bridges, pavilions, terraces and the boathouse. Olmsted handled everything else, including the planting, supervision and overall design. In May 1858, Olmsted was named the architect-in-chief of the park and Vaux served as his assistant.

'It took a massive human effort to transform the rocky and swampy site that the city had purchased in 1856 into a landscaped park. By the time Central Park was completed, workers had gone over every foot of ground, raising or lowering the surface; they had transformed natural drainage courses into artificial subterranean waterways and created the illusions of picturesque abundance and distant prospects. In the first *five years, labourers excavated, moved, or brought into the park nearly 2.5 million cubic yards of stone and earth—enough to raise the level of a football field eighty stories. With pickaxes, hammers, shovels, and 166 tons of gunpowder (more than the amount fired at the Battle of Gettysburg), they cut through more than 300,000 cubic yards of gneiss rock veined with granite. Stone-breakers crushed 35,000 cubic yards of this rock into paving stone. Contractors supplied six million bricks, 35,000 barrels of cement, 65,000 cubic yards of gravel, and 19,000 cubic yards of sand. Gardeners fertilised the ground with more than 40,000 cubic yards of manure and compost and planted 270,000 trees and shrubs. Out of this immense expenditure of labour and materials—20,000 men and $5 million by 1866—emerged the park's drives, paths, bridges, hills, lakes, lawns, and scenic vistas.'[1]*

Central Park has been restored and revitalised at various points in its more than 150-year history. The park is now managed by The Central Park Conservancy—a citizen-based Board of Guardians—which is responsible for all maintenance, fundraising and administrative functions.

1. Roy Rosenzweig and Elizabeth Blackmar, *The Park and the People: A History of Central Park*, Ithaca: Cornell University Press, 1998

'She Said—She Said'

'This, mother, this is what a park should be. It offers a newer, richer, deeper experience each time we do our annual walk through it. It sounds corny, but I always wonder what magic Olmsted and Vaux tapped into to create this wonder. I wish I had just a small sprinkle of that fairy dust when I design my own little gardens.'

'Ah, so you have heroes and dreams,' her mother said, liking the enthusiasm she heard.

'You could say that. Much admiration. But my days of hero worship are long gone,' she said.

Not sure how to read that response, her mother let it go. 'Over bridges and through tunnels, over and yonder we go,' she said instead, taking her daughter's arm as much to lean on as to offer her support.

'They're at the Roman Forum this week, you know,' she said to her mother, as they approached Cleopatra's Needle, which had its origins in Egypt, and no connection to the Roman Empire at all.

'Yes, I heard. Some father-son bonding through the annals of history?' she asked, encouraging her to open up, but not wanting to seem too inquisitive.

'Yes. They're always so wary around each other, but who knows, maybe the history of the place will help draw them out.'

Magnolia and crabapple trees were coming into spring bloom around the colossal obelisk. 'So, you and I in Central Park at this oldest outdoor monument in the city, and Paul and his dad there among the Roman ruins. A planned symmetry, of sorts?' she asked, only partly in jest.

'Perhaps. Maybe we both wanted to hear what our parents thought of our dilemma,' she said, matter-of-factly, offering as wide a berth as her mother would ever have to offer her views. And like any mother who knows not to pass up such a rare opportunity, she took it.

'It's not for me to tell you what you should do, but people can grow and change, you know, you have to give them a chance. It sometimes seems clear to me that you will be back together by the time we walk through this park next year.'

'It's not all that clear to me,' she said, scrutinizing the indecipherable hieroglyphs on the cleaned up granite surface of the ancient needle.

'You've always made a virtue of ignoring the obvious, sweetheart.'

They were now at the centre of the gently curved Bow Bridge. One of the seven original cast iron bridges in the park, most recently renovated in 1998, it had withstood the pitter-patter of millions of pedometered footsteps. They leaned over the delicate, filigree-like railing and peered into the limpid lake below.

'So many bridges. Makes you wonder what runs beneath, doesn't it? Or what gaps they're trying to span...' she mused, with a sudden sense of déjà-vu, recalling a similar question being posed at the Lodhi Garden two years before.

'I know it's been hard on you, my dear. You took up the mantle of being the responsible one, the provider. And along the way, it made you become something you hadn't planned on. Perhaps you feel transformed in a way you didn't want... Perhaps you blame him for it. '

'Do you think I'm wrong to feel that?' she asked, sensing an undercurrent of implied criticism from her mother.

'No,' said her mother. 'But you're seeing the glass half empty when I think those of us on the outside can see the glass quite robustly full, overflowing, in fact.'

'What?' she asked, annoyed.

'Too much metaphor mixing on my part, sorry,' her mother responded, realising that it was best to back off. But, continued nevertheless. 'You've really come into your own with the practice, working with Paul's dad. You've become his most trusted professional partner. And Paul, maybe it was a good thing he did in retrospect, pursuing his passion. He was honest and upfront about what he didn't want. Now he's in his element with his photography studio, and there's no competition between you on the practice. That's probably a good thing too.'

'It wasn't what we had planned,' she said softly, looking at the water flowing under the bridge.

They rested on the granite lava rock immortalised in dozens of Hollywood films.

'I've been reading a lot about this park, lately. Mainly because, you know, Olmsted. Here, listen to this,' she said, pulling out her phone.

'The only part of the Park that remains unchanged may be the granite outcroppings that helped make the land cheap. Central Park has an unusually rich endowment of exposed, ancient bedrock— rocks that are not only highly decorative, but also contain visible evidence of epochal events dating back hundreds of millions of years...The schist was formed from sedimentary shale by intense subterranean heat and pressure some 450 million years ago in the Paleozoic Era. While the schist of Umpire Rock was being formed, it was twisted and folded by upheavals in the earth's depths.'

'I suppose we're all twisted and formed by upheavals in our past,' her mother said.

'Go on...'

'Well, look, let me not trivialise what has happened. Let Paul worry about his own father. Let's talk about you and our lives. I think your father's leaving us affected you deeply. It certainly changed me as a person, and as a mother. I became more accepting that people are unknowable at some fundamental level, no matter how close they are to us. And you expect such absolute loyalty and commitment that I wonder who could ever live up to those standards. So yes, like this rock, we all contain visible evidence of past events in our lives.'

'But did you know this Umpire Rock is also called Rat Rock because it used to be swarmed by rats at night?' her daughter asked, as she digested this sudden exposition from her mother.

'Now, come on, I'm not going to suggest that we're like swarming rats!' Her mother gave her a hug and said, 'Never mind this dumb rock, look at those fluttering new leaves on the delicate branches up ahead on the right.'

'Frank Lloyd Wright said doctors bury their mistakes and architects build them,' she said, her thoughts still on that which lies buried.

Her mother, with her customary preference for clarity asked, 'Well, you're a landscape architect, so would that mean you plant your mistakes?'

'Oh, good one, mom,' she said, looking at her phone. 'How did you know to say that? Let me correct myself. What FLW actually said was, a doctor can bury his mistakes, but an architect can only advise his client to plant vines!'

'Well, either way, I think FLW was an egomaniacal, pompous ass.'

'No argument from me there. Even FLW would agree with you! But I guess what I'm trying to say, mom, is that I feel

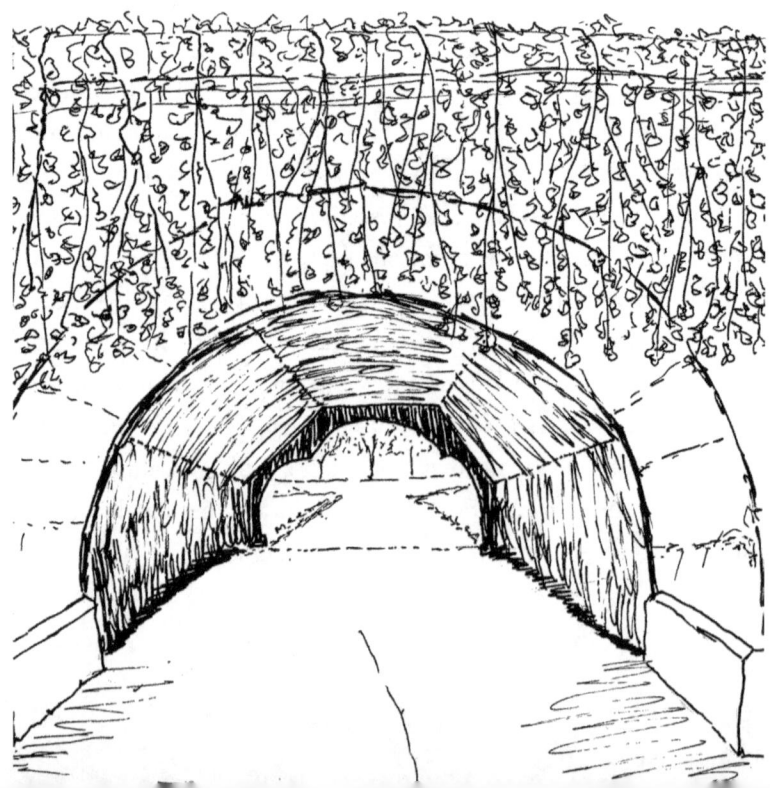

like I lost the free-spiritedness that used to be me. I should have been the one creating joyous gardens of love. And here I am instead, imposing geometry on the natural world in a sad attempt to bring order and have control. Paul should have been the one doing that, like Vaux. I should have been Olmsted!'

'Shouldn't you be having this conversation with Paul?'

'No, because I'm here now, having it with you,' she said, petulantly.

'All right, dear. But you may want to be just as expressive with him as well. It would be much more helpful. He may understand better than you think, you know.'

'Mother, please. Can you stop with the well-meaning, ill-conceived advice for once and just let me be?'

And so they walked on. Mother and daughter navigating the uneven surface between showing concern and reserving judgement.

'And here's the next bridge we need to cross,' her mother said. 'It never hurts to work it out. Or walk it out,' she added, and smiled, amused at her own twist on the phrase.

Her daughter didn't seem to have heard, and kept up a brisk pace. 'See, I noticed you sped up right there just now, to keep up with me. We can only do our walks because we keep our pace in sync. That's not the case with Paul and me. It's like he suddenly went off on his own journey, not caring about the route I had charted out. I dislike ill-considered strides.'

'Well, slow down there, girlie, I'm not as young as I once was any more. I can't match steps with you for long.' So they slowed down and took a moment to take in the presence of the skyline looming over them.

'Had you agreed on that route together though? Or did you map it out with your straight lines from point A to point B? Meandering paths can eventually lead to the same destination. I mean Paul does have a right to decide whether or not he wants to go into practice with his father...'

'Thanks. Sugarcoat it, won't you, mother?'

'Well, I'm just being honest, my dear. It's important to tell the truth when it matters.'

'Yeah, but that's not *the truth*. See my air-quotes? It's just your take on my life.'

'I don't deny it. But interpretation is still an essential part of life. Where there's truth, there are lies too. And where there's hurt there's healing too. And in sorrow there's joy.'

'Now you're going all Buddha on me,' she laughed, appreciating her mother's failed attempt at making a leap from the thorny to the new age. 'I do look back with regret at some of my behaviour and my choices, mom. It's not like I'm blind.'

'As the great Confucius said, learn from regret, but never just regret. Or was it Lao Tse?'

'It was neither, and you know it. It was your own mom-ism,' she laughed.

The Pierre and the Sherry Netherlands stood to attention, looking over the park as they had done for somewhat less than a century, but still long enough to have towered over a few lifetimes destroyed by buried resentments and unaddressed slights.

The next day they were in the park again, and how differently the garden presented itself now. What had seemed tentative and uncertain, today seemed clear and sure. Had she imagined that yesterday there had been fiery, autumn leaves still clinging to the branches? It had been by turns, too hot and just a tad too cool, a turning of seasons that couldn't quite define itself. But today it was an indisputably clear spring day. The foliage was green, fresh and new, the chill in the air was on the wane, and their vision was as clear as the blue sky above.

'So what's our walking goal for today, then?' she asked her daughter eagerly.

'I have a route picked out, with your permission,' she said, acknowledging their conversation the day before. 'It's a nice easy circuit again.'

'But we'll stop when we feel like stopping?'

'Yes, of course. Let's just say we're deliberately meandering.'

And so they calibrated their steps and walked apace along with the runners and striders, the nannies and the babies, the tourists and the lovers, the bikers and the listless wanderers.

'Sometimes one does just need to walk it out, mom, you were right,' she said, surprising her mother.

'You just have to remember that no matter how small the step, it's the only way forward. One step at a time, and then one more and another, till you're on a journey. Look back and look ahead, but keep walking, that's all there is to it. It's the same thing I said to you when you first started walking!'

'That was a long time ago, and I somehow doubt you said that.'

Her mother ignored that. 'I mean it's not like I'm saying anything profound or original. It's the same for everyone.'

'Yeah, we all learn to walk. I'm keeping track of your steps and our speed on this Fitbit, mom, let's go,' she said.

'And as always, we're booked for cocktails at the Ritz Carlton when we're done?'

'Mom, but we just got started. And it'll only be four o'clock when we get there…'

'Sure,' her mother said boldly. 'But who's going to care?'

They sped up their pace in anticipation of the awaiting watering hole.

They paused in the North Meadow Butterfly Gardens, enjoying the colourful enclosure which played host to Monarch butterflies on their migration from Mexico. Orange and black wings fluttered around the carefully planted bergamot and milkweed.

'Was it your idea, his trip to Rome?'

'Yes, sort of. Our estrangement has had some strange consequences. Ironically, I'm now closer to his dad than I am to Paul. I mean we're together every day at the office, his dad and I. And I can see how much he misses Paul. Especially because they only have each other since Sarah's passing. And Paul needs to be there for him. Just because he's set up his own shop, doesn't mean he can be completely selfish. They need each other.'

'You're speaking of Paul and his father now… They need each other? Yes, yes, they do,' her mother said, without irony.

And after a moment added, 'So you suggested that they go on a trip together and work things out. That was a good idea. And Paul was open to this idea then?'

'Yes, we've been talking more lately. We know from personal experience that holding it all in builds up a lifetime of resentments,' she acknowledged. 'Actually not one lifetime, two lives, so two lifetimes.'

'Unresolved equations do have a rippling effect on so many others down the line. Generations. I mean our behaviour patterns are like butterfly wings aren't they? It's that theory of entropy or something... No, that's not it—not entropy. Oh, what's it called?' She had begun to forget things she once could recall effortlessly.

'It's Chaos Theory, mom' she said, pulling out her phone for confirmation. 'This is from Wikipedia, sorry, but still... *The butterfly effect is the concept that small causes can have large effects. Initially, it was used with weather prediction but later the term became a metaphor used in and out of science.*'

'Hmm, yes, that's it. Thank you, Wikipedia. Chaos theory and the butterfly effect...'

Her daughter continued swiping at her phone and said, 'Here we go, from the Stanford Encyclopaedia of Philosophy, which I know you will appreciate more. *The big news about chaos is supposed to be that the smallest of changes in a system can result in very large differences in that system's behaviour. The so-called butterfly effect has become one of the most popular images of chaos. The idea is that the flapping of a butterfly's wings in Argentina could cause a tornado in Texas three weeks later.*'

'Yes, that's exactly what I meant. Father and son bristle at each other and it has an effect on all their other relationships.'

'Yup, from the drawing board all the way to the Lodhi Gardens, and the Roman Forum, to here in Central Park, and who knows, where else, we can feel those fluttering wings,' she said considering her own relationship with her estranged parents.

'Come, let's rest here for a bit on this bench. This particular
one, on this curve, overlooking the pond. There are more than
9,000 of them in the park, didn't you tell me that last year?'

'Yes, last year was all about facts and figures for me. Here is
what's listed on the park site,' she said, pointing to her phone
as they sat down.

'*There are 36 bridges and arches in Central Park.*
There are more than 9,000 benches.
The perimeter of Central Park is 6 miles.
There are 7 water bodies.
All composed on an 843 acre plot of land.'

'If you were given those specs as a kit of parts to design a park for the city, what do you think you'd have done?' her mother asked.

'I'd be sitting at my desk with colour pencils, in a state of panic at the scale of the damn project. Thank God for Olmsted! I do admire his free thinking. As I told you, I would have ruined it by trying to impose straight lines and structure. Would have ended up with the Villa d'Este instead of this paradise.'

'Well, that Italian garden is certainly magnificent and beautiful in its own way. All right, give me a hand off this bench. Let's see what more these men created.'

'Here's something else for you to ponder, mom. Vaux was the architect but it was, Olmsted, who had hardly any formal education, who ended up with the title of Chief Architect for Central Park.'

'I did not know that.'

'Olmsted was the Superintendant of the park at first and later Vaux quit the partnership. It sounds complicated. But I guess they had an on-again, off-again relationship too!'

'Yes, but it sounds like it was born of a deep and mutual understanding and respect for each other's talent and integrity.'

'I don't know how you could claim to know that, but your point is registered and noted, mom.'

'Ah, here we are, back out into the lives of others,' she said, looking at the facades on Central Park West. 'But soft, what light through yonder window breaks...'

'I remember how you used to take me for a stroll through the neighbourhood after dinner, looking into windows and watching families do whatever families do. You were such a voyeur, mother!'

It had been their ritual. Walking around the periphery of the park, they would look into the windows of apartments as they lit up at twilight. What stories echoed their own? What emotions were held in check, what anger was directed at the wrong person?

'Families no longer do what families did,' her mother said wistfully. 'And I am aware that they now call it stalking. I don't think I was being voyeuristic then, was I? We were just telling stories, wondering at the lives of others. There was no malintent. It was just my preferred alternative to reading *Goodnight Moon* every bedtime!' she laughed. 'Look, there's a young family sitting down to dinner,' she pointed to a window on the first floor as they walked past. A cat was perched on the sill. It seemed to her like only yesterday that they were that family.

'That could be Paul and I, is what you're saying. I know, mother, I'm not dumb.'

There it was—the child's need to always be at the centre of the parent's world. There was no reason to explain that her nostalgia had been for her own past. So she said, 'Neither of you is the slightest bit dumb, dear. You balance each other out so well. If only you could see it as all of us on the outside do.'

'It's always easier looking in from the outside, isn't it, mom?'

They turned back into the park then, away from the realities of complex, real lives. 'According to the Park Conservancy site, there is a clear "intent" behind every space that's designed here. I find that such a juxtaposition! To be able to camouflage that intentional design and create a natural garden. Oh, the enormity of such a mind. I can't help it, mom, it gets me every time. For me, being here is like being in the presence of the divine.' She was in her element now, landscape architect one hundred percent.

'I know what you mean, my dear. Can we chart our lives with such intent and create such subtle beauty?'

'Yes,' she said, slowing down to listen.

'Well, I know I gave up in my forties, when your father left and I saw that nothing was going as I had planned. Before that, I would always script ahead. But then I figured, why struggle to keep the colours inside the lines? Better to draw shapes around the colours.'

'But I'm lost without a plan,' she said simply, pointing to the mapped route of their walk on her phone. 'I panic, it's just too scary. That's why I always impose symmetry. Luckily Paul's dad likes precision and geometry and loves my work. Exactly the opposite of Olmstead. Did you know there's only one straight line in Central Park? And Vaux did that.'

'For me, the pleasure of being here is to be lost! The thing about gardens is that you can get lost in them.'

'Intentionally lost, or lost-lost?'

'Purposefully lost.'

'Yes, I agree, that's precisely the appeal of this park. But being lost is entirely an illusion! How subtly Olmsted buried his intent by planting vines around it!'

'One might say that about each of our lives. We all create and believe our own illusions.'

'I've been meaning to ask, what is the difference between pastoral and picturesque?'

'Hmm, let me think. Pastoral spaces are purposefully designed to provide a sense of openness and expansiveness. They are spaces for quiet reflection, reading, or admiring the surrounding scenery. Wow, I never thought I would remember that from LA Theory 101!'

'And picturesque?'

They settled onto another bench overlooking the vast expanse of green that spread out before them like a carpet. It soothed the eye and yet made them want to sprint across like a pair of newborn lambs.

'Does picturesque mean something more than pretty as a picture and beautiful, in landscape architecture?'

'Well, according to this site, *Olmsted thought picturesque landscapes were meant to create a degree of obscurity not absolutely impenetrable, but sufficient to affect the imagination with a sense of mystery.*'

'Your Olmsted really was a very wise man. Life is all of that, isn't it? Beautiful, impenetrable, mysterious, designed…'

'Yes, and finite.' She read on: '*When Olmsted and Vaux entered a proposal for the design of Central Park, the "Greensward Plan," their canvas was a desolate, rocky plot of more than 700 acres interrupted by swamps, steep ravines, and clay pits. The plot (later expanded to 840 acres) was occupied by several settlements, most prominently Seneca Village, one of the city's few middle-class black communities. There were also graveyards, which were never exhumed.'*

'Graveyards,' she repeated softly. 'The Lodhi Gardens are a bunch of tombs, the Roman Forum was originally an Etruscan burial ground, even the weird Hanging Gardens in Mumbai were built to protect the reservoir from the Tower of Silence near it.'

'How interesting—and how wonderful. Literally destruction and creation. The cycle of life and death,' her mother said, oddly delighted by the notion of graveyards serving as the canvas for reincarnation.

'Central Park was to have a Board of Guardians. What a beautiful concept, that a park should have a group of private citizens who cared for its welfare like they would that of a child who needs to be nurtured. It's evolved into the Central Park Conservancy now, which doesn't have quite the same ring,' she said, wiping away sudden tears.

'May we speak of the elephant in the room now, my dear?'

'You mean the wild cat in the garden?' she asked, pointing at the bronze crouching cougar sculpture.

'Yes, this creature that creeps up ever so suddenly on you, makes you sad. You wanted children and he broke away from your plan, left you hanging in a way, without any indication of when he would be ready. There I've said it. Perhaps he's ready now? It's been what, two years?'

'A little less than that, depending on how you count,' she said, not all that concerned with order and precision now.

'You must find a way to make that life. I want to look through the window and see the two of you, perhaps three or even four—and a cat—gathered around your dinner table.'

'I'm finally feeling like we may get there yet. I think we're ready.'

'Amen to that. Nobody ever knows what goes on inside a marriage. I always said that to you, in those early days, didn't I? But the two of you must always be self aware. That's what matters.'

At the Bethesda Terrace, she said, 'Olmsted wrote of this as an "open-air reception hall for the people." For some reason, this architecture makes me think of them in Rome.'

'But this here is based on Versailles, not Rome, even I know that!'

'I know, I know. It's European anyway, I suppose…' she said quickly, knowing full well that it was just an excuse to bring up what had been gnawing at her.

'Have you checked on them? Any word?' her mother asked, not missing a beat and wanting to avoid making her self-conscious.

'No, I don't like to interfere. He will talk to me when he's ready. Did you know he quotes Leonard Cohen when he needs help expressing himself?' she laughed.

'Ah, poets. What would our world be without them?'

'Gardeners and poets. The true romantics in this world.'

They admired the arches and paving, watched people milling about the fountain. Then she said, 'Olmsted thought nature was a civilizing influence. Well, not just him. It's been a generally held notion through the ages. Either nature is wild and needs to be tamed, or contradictorily, nature is the taming, soothing force for the human soul.'

'And clearly you would be among those wanting to tame it?'

They entered the grand vista of the Literary Walk.

'Here it is. Vaux's geometry. This mall is the only straight line in the park, emphasised by quadruple rows of American elms.'

'Sort of refreshing actually, to have this grand view down the centre. No fuss, no muss.'

'You know the story or urban myth, perhaps, right, of how the diagonal caused a rift between Mondrian and Kandinsky? And that was conceptually, still a straight line among straight lines, just going across rather than parallel or at a right angle,' she pointed out.

'They should have invested as much conviction into their personal lives,' her mother said with exasperation at the stubborn nature of the artistic temperament. 'Those two should have tried to be better friends rather than focussing on some esoteric nonsense.'

Knowing that they had both reached the limits of their walking for the day, she offered, 'Here we are then, just as planned. Cocktails at the Ritz-Carlton for you.'

They settled at the table they had reserved at the Club Lounge, to celebrate the end of their annual walking tradition. High up in the sky, with floor to ceiling windows overlooking the park, they ordered gin and tonics. It was only four in the afternoon but nobody batted an eyelid. Every table had a happy drink on it. Ah, the joys of a life well-lived. Or of being a tourist. They sipped the refreshing fizziness of their drinks and surveyed the once upon a time swamps, ravines, clay-pits and settlements.

Cars entered the park and disappeared into the forest before exiting across town. All they could see were treetops, foliage and greenery. It came as close to nature as they could imagine. 'Tamed wilderness,' she said. 'The earth truly was his canvas.'

'This here is from the Atlantic Magazine,' she said, still reading from her phone. 'One of his most remarkable technical achievements in Central Park was to make its four major crosstown thoroughfares disappear: He sunk them into the ground and hid them with foliage. Much of the park's charm derives from the alternation of rolling expanses and hidden passages, such as those that thread through the Ramble, which create the illusion of privacy and mystery.'

'Olmsted—the master of illusion. It certainly takes a lot of artifice to create natural scenery.'

'Yes it does. And living a deluded existence has its own particular charm,' they agreed.

'Now put away that phone,' her mother said.

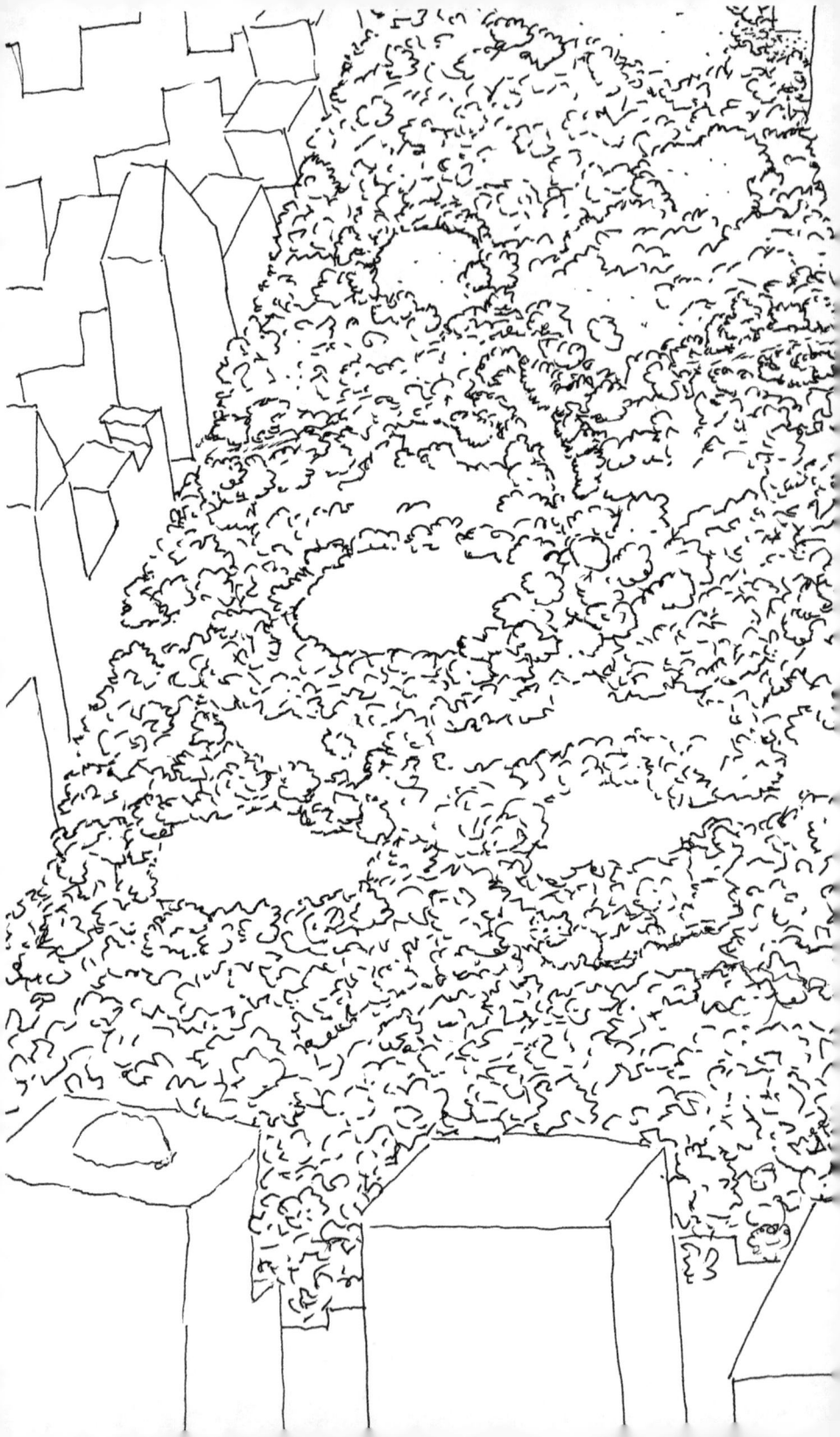

'How different it looks from here, surveying it from up above,' her mother marvelled.

'Paul's dad always laments the bird's eye view,' she said. 'He says that gardens, by definition, are tactile and must be experienced, and conceived that way too. Right from the sound of pathways, stepping on rocks and crunching gravel underfoot, to the hugging of a tree trunk. One should be able to look up at the sky beyond the foliage. Feel one's smallness in the grandeur of nature. Not look down from above.'

'Oh my. Your love for landscape architecture is deep indeed!' her mother laughed, enjoying the return of joy in her daughter's outlook.

They sipped their drinks and returned their gaze to the scene before them.

'To Olmsted and Vaux. Because who's to say which of them actually did and drew and designed what about which part of the park.'

'Yes, once again, who actually knows what is said and done by whom in a partnership. Point well hammered in now, mom.'

'Good, because for once, I wasn't actually making any point! I was just fawning over this lovely garden before us. To Olmsted and Vaux, may they be united forever!' she said, raising her glass.

'Oddly, there's no statue of either Olmsted or Vaux in the park.'

'No, but there's one of Alice in Wonderland and Simon Bolivar.'

'To the absurd!' she said, taking a large gulp.

They had already planned their return the following year to evaluate the absurd delusions they would be living then.

Hanging Gardens

MUMBAI

The Hanging Gardens, also known as Pherozeshah Mehta Gardens were created in 1881. Situated atop Malabar Hill in South Mumbai, they overlook the Arabian Sea and the necklace of Marine Drive. The terraced gardens were built over one of the city's main water reservoirs to protect it from being polluted, perhaps from the Tower of Silence that lies nearby. The gardens were laid out by Ulhas Ghapokar, about whom not much is known.

The Hanging Gardens and Kamala Nehru Park, just across on the western slope of Malabar Hill are sometimes considered to be a single entity and people, including our protagonists, often—erroneously—refer to both jointly as the Hanging Gardens. The many trees and plantings of the gardens are overshadowed by the numerous topiary animals that line the red clay pathways. The flower clock is another colourful draw. But perhaps the best-known attraction of the gardens is the Old Woman's Shoe, or the Boot House—a brightly painted, large bricks and mortar structure into which children can climb.

The Hanging Gardens are dedicated to Pherozeshah Mehta, a prominent Parsi political leader, activist and lawyer, who was called the Lion of Bombay. Mehta served as the president of Bombay Municipality four times (1884, 1885, 1905 and 1911) and was also the president of the Indian National Congress in 1890.

The gardens were last renovated in 1921 and are maintained by the Bombay Municipal Corporation, which in 2016, announced a plan for another major renovation.

'He Said—She Said'

*H*e arrived early, as always. Some things never change. He still hated being late. This time he arrived more than just early, he arrived a whole hour before the appointed time. It was a deliberate choice. He needed to do this alone before she arrived. They had planned this meeting last month, as a coming full circle to the country in which their paths had first crossed. There was an unspoken hope that they might return to New York together.

At the bottom of the steps, looking up, it all came rushing back. It was the grandparents with their little grandson that did it. He was flooded with images of the time when he had been that boy, when he had scampered over this sea of steps holding his grandfather's strong, reassuring hand, been enveloped in his grandmother's soft flesh as she hugged him to her when he fell. Up what had seemed like a wondrous pathway into an enchanted world. How simple life had been.

He was here to retrace that long ago memory, see what lessons there were still to be learned.

His grandparents had been young then too, undaunted by the mountain they had to climb. In recent years, he recalled his grandmother turning down invitations if there were more than three steps to negotiate.

'I'll carry you up them,' he had offered, and indeed done so a few times, until at the very end, when she had snorted at him in anger, 'Put me down! I am not a child to be carried.'

His grandfather would follow him at a brisk pace when he ran over the tamped down, red earth pathways. 'Slow down!' 'Stay close!' 'You'll fall!' they both shouted after him. He wished there was still someone who would worry about him scraping a knee or having his heart broken now. But there was nobody left, to carry him home at the end of the day.

'I want to see the giraffe... and then the elephant!' he had beseeched, much like the little girl who ran past him now.

'Yes, yes, we will visit all the animals,' his grandmother would say, with the patience she had never had for her own children.

He looked at the topiary now. A strangely crude menagerie that was lush during the monsoons and scrawny most of the year. But he appreciated the opportunity to see the twig skeletons underneath. What was it that lay beneath the deceptive softness above? Was this nest of sticks still a monkey in April? What about the giraffe in June? And what about this scraggly mahout riding an elephant—was this straw man still a man if he couldn't hold on to the one relationship that truly mattered?

The green arcaded walk. A tunnel of other-worldly delights. Shaded from the sun. Sheltered from the rain. Grandparents on either side. Safe, secure, without a care.

This was the spot where his grandmother would rest. She would perch on the edge of the bench, watching after them as he and Grandpa disappeared down the path. And she would be watching still, searching the crowds when they returned half an hour later.

He sat on that bench now, next to a wary cat, waiting. It was an art in itself—the ability to hold oneself in that state of anticipation. But there was still almost an hour to go, if he accounted for her chronic lateness. His anxiety was compounded by the dispersed laughter of strangers that hung around him like the fog of distant fairy dust.

Restless under the distrustful glare of the cat with her flicking tail, he conceded the bench to her reign and made his way to the inevitable destination of anyone who visits the Hanging Gardens, a destination as quixotic as the name of the garden itself.

The Shoe House. It intimidated him, though he had never let anyone know it.

There was an old woman who lived in a shoe. She terrified him. *She had so many children, she didn't know what to do.* What *did* she do finally?

The shoe obviously belonged to one of those giants who haunted him, the colossus of a frustrated old woman with too many children, who would stomp upon this hanging garden and crush it in an instant with her giant stride. He had known it then and it made him nervous now.

Up in the tiny concrete balcony, leaning over to find his grandfather who waited patiently below, and waved to him reassuringly, he would turn around and rush back down, out of the giant shoe house. A surreptitious glance back led him to imagine giant fingers threading the holes with the aglet while an enormous booming voice sang,

Come inside
Close it tight so we can hide
Over the mountain
And around we go
Here's my arrow
And here's my bow!

And the question which had always befuddled him—where was the knot in this massive shoelace? Had the old woman not taught any of the children to tie their shoes?

Who had taught him to tie his shoelaces? His kindergarten teacher, who was long gone too. She had been a kind lady. One among many kind women in his life who had helped him along the way. Tied his laces, fed him, shared a house or a laugh. And one particularly kind one who had broken his heart. Or had he broken hers? Did it matter now? He would find out soon enough.

He stirred about in the gazebo, watching the crowds. No grandparents with grandchildren now. Just a few self-conscious couples and the random Romeo staring at them. He hadn't seen that many children here after all, and certainly very few with grandparents. Odd, considering that sixty percent of India's population was now under the age of thirty. The children should have been everywhere. Was it because grandchildren no longer spent time with their grandparents? Or was it just that most were probably indoors playing video games. He was glad they didn't have children to compound their complicated lives. What a shoddy model of marriage he would have presented anyway. He blamed himself. He was a selfish jerk. Even here in this gazebo he wanted to kick out the few people around him. He wanted to wallow in his own self-indulgent melancholy.

Yes, he was *that* selfish. In a city like Mumbai, he was selfish enough to want solitude.

Pre-monsoon clouds gathered overhead and as the sky darkened, the crowds thinned out. The foliage took on a life of its own. Here was a bougainvillea creeper, all tangled and knotted, writhing and resplendent in fuchsia and saffron. Defiant and complex, engrossed in its own internal struggle, oblivious to the relentless passage of time and those who were ravaged by it. Yes, he could appreciate the troubled beauty of such an existence.

He recalled a similarly co-dependent bougainvillea in the Lodhi Gardens, years ago. This was déjà-vu. He had questioned the word 'coexisting' then, suggesting that parasitic might be a more apt term. It wasn't, she had clarified. They were symbiotic, the tree and the creeper lived happily together. But did they let each other be what each of them needed to be, he had wondered. What word would she choose today, to describe the relationship?

Pherozeshah Mehta, barrister-at-law, after whom the garden is named. There he stood, imperious, surveying the kitsch manifestation of this garden which bore his name but was now better known by the gerund verb which preceded it. Why were there elephants and giraffes along the railings and why the bizarre topiary? There were no animals here, never had been, this was no zoo. An occasional monkey and the stray dogs and cats, but what kangaroo would venture across the seas to this urban anomaly? How would Mr Mehta, he of the knighthood and law practice feel about it all? It was said that the garden pathways, seen from the air, spelled out his monogram PMG, in old-fashioned cursive, too.

He had no way to verify this but if it were true, how much more contrived could this garden get?

Away from the greenery and flowers, he was with the wild topiary and enchanted gazebo with the echoing whispers. He was no longer the little boy he had been the last time he was here. He could have been a father by now, carrying his child home after the shoe house had terrified him and the ice cream bar had lulled him into slumber. But here he was instead, sad and alone. How had this happened?

'Does anyone ever understand the life they live?' someone had once asked in a novel he had read. A novel by an author he enjoyed who had then unnecessarily waded into dystopian fiction and ruined it all. But he still wrote lines such as this. Did anyone truly understand their own life? There was time still for him to atone, to make amends, to choose another path. Not twelve steps, just two would suffice.

And here it was, the proverbial fork in the road. As advised by Yogi Berra, he took it, rushing so he could be outside when she arrived. The cold grey, rock-hewn steps led him away, offering a neutral face to what might have been a momentous decision. Rock everlasting, smoothed by erosion, sometimes shiny with the oil of a million caressing fingers. Rocks didn't consider anything of much consequence and realising this, he felt himself shrink. Just an inscrutable speck in the universe, irrelevant to the great forces that governed it. That offered a freedom as well, perhaps it was not so much a momentous choice as an obvious one.

'One step at a time,' his grandfather would have advised.

'Yes, Grandpa, I've got it now.'

'Be careful, watch your step, don't fall,' his grandmother would add.

'I won't this time, Grandma.'

He was no longer a little boy. He would get it right this time.

And back he went to lean against the low wall, as he had in another garden at another time, sort-of-waiting while he nibbled on a Kwality orange bar which now cost significantly more and tasted not quite as good.

She pulled up in a black and yellow taxi, just past the hour. Almost on time, by her standards. And he found it didn't bother him quite as much, to be kept waiting any more. Maybe it was just the waiting for her that he didn't mind.

'Sorry, I tried...' she began.

'Doesn't matter. Taffy-time,' he shrugged. 'Stretches to fit everything in.'

She looked puzzled but said nothing, just looked at him a little more closely instead.

She took off her sandals, as was her wont in gardens, and in they went.

'The old woman must have been their grandmother. Nobody describes a mother with so many children as being old,' she said.

'Grandma? Really? I never quite...'

'What fun it must have been for all those grandkids to be racing around the shoe house with a sweet old grandma who didn't know what to do with them. I bet she did what all grandmas do—hugged them and cooked and fed them all sorts of treats.'

So this is how worlds collide, he thought. His anxiety began to lift as he looked at the concrete boot anew. Children and adults were all over it, laughing, posing for photos, amused and distracted from their daily cares.

'That claustrophobic balcony though...'

She looked at him as though he was speaking of something else entirely. 'That little overhang? Oh, can't you just see the grandmother waving at all the children from up there? Low enough off the ground to be able to see each one of them as they leave at the end of their summer breaks. She must have shed a few tears there in that little balcony—sad to see them go, but glad for having had them with her for a while.'

He recalled his own summer break and saying goodbye to his grandparents. How his grandmother had hugged him to her then. 'Come back again soon,' she said. 'You'll be as tall as your grandpa the next time I see you.'

How had she turned this garden experience upside down all of a sudden? Was this the same garden he had just wandered through with equal measures of anxiety and melancholy?

'That shoelace, though…' he said, with a fair degree of trepidation.

'Oh it must be based on that cute bunny ears song from kindergarten. Did you ever learn it at yours?' And she recited:

'Over, under, around and through,
Meet Mr Bunny Rabbit, pull and through.'

He remembered it now. The bunny, even if a giant one, was a much more appealing apparition than the intimidating giants that he imagined in all sorts of scenarios.

'It's a much better rhyme, the one about being shut inside a tepee and going over some mountain than the one they taught at my school.'

'I love this shoe house, trite as it is. I just don't like the concrete, makes it cold inside. But then again, that's the building material here, it's solid and it sure handles the weather well.'

'Oh my gosh, look at all these kids scampering through this gazebo. Have you noticed how many children there are everywhere? Just all over the place,' she sighed. Was it annoyance or yearning?

There were indeed. How come he hadn't seen so many in his round through here just an hour ago?

'They come here later in the evening when it cools off and they've finished their homework, you know. All parks have designated times for designated users. It's an unwritten code. You can decipher it if you pay attention to the patterns. We had it down to a science at the Lodhi Gardens, remember?'

Yes, he remembered it well. How could he forget?

'Look at this tree trunk.'

They measured themselves against it and found that they barely made it above the roots.

'What a giant of a tree, growing so quietly here. Like a great benevolent spirit watching over the chaos we create at its feet.'

'A benevolent giant that treads like a colossus among us.'

'At Lodhi you thought all the tree trunks were damsels in diaphanous clothing there for your delight.'

'I'm not seeing any damsels now,' he said, just to clarify.

'No? Is that good or bad?'

'It's good,' he said, after a pause. 'But let me correct myself, I am seeing one. Come, I want to show you another tree.'

'We can be like this. Inseparable,' he stated, unafraid.

'Growing old and beautiful together?'

'You think we could pull it off?' They walked around the gnarly, resplendent bougainvillea. 'Was I really as cold as stone? Were you really as nurturing as this tree that lets the creeper grow upon her?'

They stopped to consider this. 'No and no. I know that now. We're not stone and tree,' she said. 'We were just too bewildered to know any better.'

He turned to look at her. This wasn't quite what he had dared to expect. Something had changed. There was a fundamental shift of mood. But he had spent the last couple of years ruing the way he had walked away. 'I did make some mistakes.'

'Hey, look, so did I,' she stated bluntly. 'But we've had some time to ponder over what we did, haven't we?'

'Nothing quite like the agony of regret.'

'Some angst is necessary, of course. Into every life a little rain must fall.'

As if on cue, a few raindrops pattered gently to the ground and settled the dust around them.

How quickly situations can go from despair to elation. Did he dare disturb the universe so?

'You don't find it crude? This ridiculous topiary, this quite banal layout, the unappealing entrance?'

'Not the words I'd choose at all. Maybe it's a matter of perspective. But just think of what lies beneath! These gardens cover a reservoir which holds billions of gallons of water for the city. They hang on Malabar Hill as a lid to keep the water clean.'

She paused for effect, before adding, 'We are walking upon water! How wondrous is that? The fantastical animals make sense to me that way. This is a wonderland, really.'

'Lucky Pherozeshah Mehta to have the garden named after him, then. A legacy he probably neither expected nor aspired to.'

'Wasn't he a lawyer with Lokmanya Tilak or something? I read that somewhere. He accepted knighthood from the British government in India and was considered a sell-out by some,' she said, having looked up all the facts about the park, as she loved to do.

'There's an alternate view. My grandfather told me about him, he admired him quite a bit for being a true liberal among the leaders of the Independence. You can see how that would have appealed to grandpa. Pherozeshah Mehta's legacy has to do with keeping the extremist thinkers from taking over the agenda of the Indian National Congress. He had nothing to do with the water supply of Bombay or landscape architecture, though,' he added.

'Yeah. Who knows how we'll be remembered when we're gone. If we're fortunate enough to be remembered at all,' she said. 'I mean for all that naming, the statue there isn't even that of Pherozeshah Mehta. It's of a Seth Anandilal Podar, for his services to the city.'

'What? No...' he said, incredulous, looking again at the back of the grand statue.

'Yeah, didn't you read the huge plaque on the front of the pedestal? It states Podar's name and explains how his statue came to be placed there in 1947.'

'No, I didn't read the history. I resist reading facts and dates, for some reason. Anyway, my father believes our miniscule lives are inconsequential against the grandeur of civilizations which are ultimately judged only by their monumental remains.'

'This from your trip to the Roman Forum?'

'Yes. But not just the physical remains, also the ideas, the intellectual heft of a civilization is what matters.' He stopped. 'It's what matters—to my father, I mean.'

'I think he's much more sensitive than you give him credit for, Paul. I've seen him up close these past two years, and he— and my mother too—think we belong together. And perhaps they're not wrong?'

They left that hanging in the garden, not wanting to disturb the clear indication that something was certainly being rebuilt here.

'But what of poor old Ulhas Ghapokar who laid the gardens out in 1880?' she asked, when they stopped to look back at he who was not Pherozeshah Mehta, aloft upon his pedestal. 'He's the true unsung hero here. There's no information about him out there other than that somebody named him on Wikipedia. I did a search. Ulhas Ghapokar. Nothing.'

'How do we know for sure that he actually designed it then? That he even existed?'

'You mean someone just made up a name like Ulhas Ghapokar?' she laughed.

That sound, that joy, that face, he felt like picking her up and putting her on that pedestal. Who cared about Ulhas. Or some knighted lawyer. Or even a leaping kangaroo upon a railing.

'There's so much I want to say,' he blurted out. Unable to articulate further, he relied on his good-for-every-situation fallback. '*If you want to strike me down in anger, here I stand, I'm your man.*'

'You still quote Leonard Cohen!' she laughed. 'But wait, do you mean that? You're saying you'll stand up and be there for me, no matter what? In joy and despair, in victory and defeat, for better or worse, you'll be my man?'

'Yes, it's what I said,' he replied, not hesitating for a second. He felt his father would have approved.

They walked on, quiet, until he said, 'I've always worried about using language. A wrong word here or there feels like it could be disastrous. I blame my mother for it. I miss showing her my photographs and hearing her turn words into poetry.'

'I know you miss her. Your dad sometimes tells me about little things you'd all do together. He even told me about the trip to Rome when you were seven!'

'My mother loved you, you know,' he said. 'She thought you were the bee's knees. She loved that phrase!'

She laughed, recognising that they were on the brink of something. 'I intuit much too much from body language and signals that are too ethereal to be explained. I blame my father for that, as I do for so many things. I blame him for all my failures,' she laughed.

'*I love your solitude and I love your pride.*'

'Him again?' she smiled. 'But do you?'

'No,' he said. 'No, I hate both. I hate how your need for aloneness enforces solitude upon me. And I hate how your pride distances you from expressing your needs.'

'Why didn't you say so in the Lodhi Gardens when we were there? Thoughts like these—solitude and pride—are so much better suited to the solemn monuments of that garden…'

'…and so unsuited to the kitschy nature of the park we're in,' he finished for her.

'You can still finish my sentences,' she said without much surprise and a fair degree of contentment.

'Yes, I want to always be the one who finishes your sentences,' he said, getting kitschy himself.

She didn't hesitate for a moment. 'Then it's now or never. You need to say something to me urgently.'

And so he leapt across continents and centuries for help from an English poet to say what had been left hanging in this and every other garden they had been in.

'*Grow old along with me, the best is yet to be.*'

'Yes,' she accepted.

Was it this simple? Had it always been?

He took her hand and they walked past the little topiary elephant rider who looked fat and happy this time around, while the giraffe looked over them and laughed.

Author's Note

A small story set in the Lodhi Garden, written and illustrated twenty-five years ago, lay in a box and journeyed around the world. It wasn't until my parents asked about it last year that I found it, yellowing on typed paper with pasted, photocopied images of the garden, tucked away among old drawings from architecture school. And so the journey of two characters begun a quarter of a century ago developed as they travelled through gardens, reflecting on their lives.

All the illustrations were done with Rotring Isographs on acid free drawing paper. It is a dying art, and those of a certain generation know the pleasure of marking a vellum sheet with that chrome-plated, stainless steel tip.

I would like to thank Jatin Lad for photographing the illustrations and bringing them to life on the page. His patience and advice on all matters visual has been invaluable. Alka Samant, graphic designer and friend, has been generous with her time and a great companion for discussions about paper and paint. I am grateful to Maithili Doshi and Rajinder Ganju for helping with the book design. And a big thank you to Renuka Chatterjee for seeing the potential in that lone Lodhi story.